Editor Louisa Sladen
Editor-in-Chief John C. Miles
Designer Heather Billin/Billin Design Solutions
Art Director Jonathan Hair

© 2001 Moira Butterfield

The right of Moira Butterfield to be identified
as the author of this work has been asserted.

First published in 2001
by Franklin Watts
96 Leonard Street
London
EC2A 4XD

Franklin Watts Australia
56 O'Riordan Street
Alexandria
NSW 2015

ISBN 0 7496 4255 6 (hbk)
0 7496 4417 6 (pbk)

Dewey classification: 942.05

A CIP catalogue record for this book is available
from the British Library.

Printed in Great Britain

The diary of
A YOUNG
ELIZABETHAN ACTOR

by Moira Butterfield
Illustrated by Brian Duggan

W
FRANKLIN WATTS
LONDON•SYDNEY

ALL ABOUT THIS BOOK

English theatre became famous in the sixteenth and seventeenth centuries during the reign of Queen Elizabeth I and then King James I. Playwrights such as William Shakespeare and Ben Jonson wrote plays that are still world famous today. By law, women were not allowed to act, so boys took the female parts in plays. This story is about a boy actor called Will Savage, and the events of his life during the last few years of Elizabeth I's reign.

WHAT WE KNOW

Although this story is imaginary, the details are based on what we know about life at the time. The story mentions real events such as the Earl of Essex's rebellion, the performance of *Richard the Second* by Shakespeare's acting company, and their appearances at Lord Hunsdon's house and Queen Elizabeth's court. The plays that Will performs were ones that modern historians know were performed at the time. Although the original Globe Theatre no longer exists, historians have pieced together how it might have looked using old sketches and documents. A replica of the Globe Theatre has now been built near the original site.

A DIFFERENT LANGUAGE

Although Will Savage would have spoken English, he would have spoken and written it differently to the way we do now. He would have used different expressions and phrases, some of which would be hard for a modern person to understand. That's why this story has been written in language used nowadays.

TO FIND OUT MORE...

At the back of this book there is some more information on how plays were staged in Elizabethan times. There is also a timeline which shows important events which took place during Shakespeare's life, and a glossary that explains the meaning of unusual words used in this book.

I dedicate this diary to my dear sister Judith,
who lives a quiet and blameless life in the fair
English town of Marlborough.
I hope that one day she will read this and
treasure it as a true record of the life of her
youngest brother as a boy player with the
Chamberlain's Men company of actors upon
the stage of the Globe Theatre, London.

Begun in the year 1600, during the glorious
reign of good Queen Elizabeth.

Will Savage

 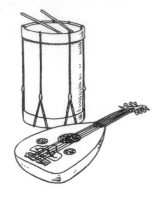

1 SEPTEMBER 1600

Dearest Judith, this diary is for you.

You always said you would love to be a player on the stage but since women are banned from such work it can never be, so until my voice breaks it is I, your youngest brother, who leads the life of an actor playing female parts.

I know you would act beautifully if you were only allowed to, but there is nothing to be done except paint a picture of my life in words so that you will be able, perhaps, to imagine yourself in my place, speaking my lines in front of a theatre crowd.

When I have filled this book with my jottings I will visit you to hand it over myself. Until that happy day I will try my best to write in its pages regularly.

4 SEPTEMBER 1600

Don't think the life of a player is all easy fame, dear sister. Either we are working every hour of daylight to please the London crowds, or we're on tour, trotting along some muddy back road in the country with only the cows for company.

I have just returned to London after a summer spent travelling with my acting master, Mr Heminges, together with some of the other actors from the Globe. To be honest I was glad to be out of the stinking London streets, fit only for rats and beggars in July and August. At this time of the year they are strewn with rotting rubbish that steams in the sunshine. The heat sometimes spreads deadly diseases. The theatres are ordered to close for two months in case plague spreads through the crowds.

Besides, the summer travelling brought back sweet memories. I saw many a young boy running helter-skelter up the street when they saw us setting up the stage in their town square. You know well I was once such a boy.

Do you remember when the Chamberlain's Men came to Marlborough? It is still so clear in my mind it seems like yesterday, though in truth it was three years ago and I was only thirteen. I sat as close as I could to the makeshift stage, unable to take my eyes off the players.

Then long after the performance was over I followed them around and made myself a confounded nuisance until Mr Heminges agreed to try me out on some singing, dancing and line-reading. Of course my reading was good from all the grammar school learning that Mother insisted on, God rest her soul.

"We need boys like you in our acting company, Will," said Mr Heminges. "You have a fine feeling for the stage, I can tell. Do you want to be a player?"

"I'd love that more than anything in the world!" I replied, and so, as you know, Mr Heminges went to find Father, who was busy at work in the apothecary shop. Mr Heminges suggested I be apprenticed as an actor for three years.

"Your boy will get no finer training than the one I will give him, and he'll be performing with the Chamberlain's Men, the finest acting company in London. He shall live at my house at my expense and I shall teach him his business. I'll give you £8 for him if his mother will agree."

With so many children to feed and so little room in the cottage, Father didn't hesitate for long. "His mother is dead these past two years. So £8 it is. The boy has a quick wit. Let him use it!"

Do you remember hearing it all, as you hid behind the door? I remember you cried to think I was leaving, and I promised to send you lace and ribbons from London if you dried your tears.

6 SEPTEMBER 1600

So now, Judith, it's time for work, for the summer is gone and the new acting season has begun at the Globe Theatre. Every afternoon at two of the clock we act our latest tale for the audience, who have been ferried by boat from the City of London across the River Thames to Bankside, where our theatre stands. Some of them will be rowed home again before it gets dark, and some will linger in the Bankside taverns, bear-baiting pits and whorehouses, and end up sleeping in a hedge!

Audience and acting company alike pray for good weather. On stage, we actors are sheltered from a downpour by a roof that juts out above our heads. The richer sort of playgoers stay under cover in wooden galleries set around the theatre walls. But people who can only afford a penny entrance fee must stand on the ground in front of the stage, open to whatever the clouds may throw at them. We call them groundlings. Sometimes they look quite comically bedraggled and it's at times like this they grow extra-loud and we hear impatient shouts: "Get a move on up there! I'm drowning!" and "This play is as dull as the weather!" We smell them as well as hear them. A damp audience stinks like a herd of goats.

I should sleep now. Tomorrow I will rehearse in the morning for one play, then act in another one in the afternoon. Now do you see what hard work it is? But despite this I never tire of it, not from the day I first saw the crowd smiling up at me as I stood on the stage.

12 SEPTEMBER 1600

I have promised to write you a true account of my days here, which means the bad as well as the good. Well, though I love being one of the Chamberlain's Men, I am feeling more and more frustrated. When the leader of our company, Richard Burbage, gives out the parts for a new play I always seem to get the supporting female roles, never the grandest lady with the longest speeches. It happened again today. I got two parts for our next play – a servant girl, and a goddess who pops down through the trapdoor in the roof above the stage and says: "That's it. The play's over. They all lived happily ever after."

There are four boy apprentices at the Globe and competition is tough, but I know I could handle bigger female roles if only they'd let me. Time is running out. I'm nearly sixteen and my voice could break soon… Then what? My greatest wish is to go on to the male adult parts, but to do that I must prove my acting abilities now.

I have asked Mr Heminges about it and he thinks my acting is fine but I'm held back because I am shorter than the other boys, and so I'm very useful for playing children and minor female roles. He has promised to talk to Mr Burbage about giving me a better chance.

20 SEPTEMBER 1600

Our new season goes well so far. We are a very strong acting company, I think, because our best actors hold shares in the theatre itself (Mr Heminges is one of these). Between them, they pay to put the plays on and each takes a slice of the profits, so they are always keen to keep the standards high and the theatre filled up.

One of the "sharers" is our playwright, William Shakespeare, who writes parts for each of the actors according to their special skill. For instance, some are good at playing kings and soldiers, while others are better at clowning. As I said, I seem to be pigeonholed as a child or a minor female.

With this in mind I took my courage in my hands today and found Mr Shakespeare backstage in the tiring room, where the actors change. I don't know him well and I've never dared speak to him about my acting before, but he seemed in a jolly enough mood: "Hello, Will. A fine name, if I may say so!" He has a kindly face, Mr Shakespeare, and a bald head that he has a habit of patting as he thinks. I jumped right in and told him how I felt.

"So you'd like a starring role written especially for you, would you? Not asking much, then!" His eyes wrinkled at the corners as he smilingly replied.

"Your master, Mr Heminges, has already spoken to me about you. I told him I can't promise anything, but I'll see what I can do." I was so relieved I believe I did a little jig, and Mr Shakespeare laughed. He took a bit of time with me then, to find out more about my life. He asked me about my childhood and smiled when he heard I had been to grammar school.

"I was at grammar school, too. In Stratford," he told me. "But like you, I heeded the call of the stage. I still go back to Stratford; I have a wife and family there. But they have had to accept that the heart of theatre beats here in London, so this is where I must live and work."

So you see, the great William Shakespeare is quite human after all, and his kindness has given me some hope for the future. If my voice holds out and he writes a really good part just for me, then I'll be able to show everyone how well I can act.

24 SEPTEMBER 1600

We have had alarming news about the future of the theatre! A black cloud of tension is forming, reaching towards the Globe from Queen Elizabeth's court. The reason is that the Queen's old favourite, the Earl of Essex, is in disgrace and Mr Shakespeare is a well-known Essex supporter. I believe Essex has been a patron of his – giving him financial help – and Mr Shakespeare has even been known to put speeches into his plays that glorify this important friend of his.

Essex was once the Queen's favourite, but he disobeyed her orders when fighting in Ireland, and was put under house arrest. In August he was freed, but banned from showing his face at court. He is very angry at his treatment and is suspected of plotting some kind of revenge against the Queen's new advisors, whom he hates. If these advisors assume that the Chamberlain's Men are supporting Essex and whatever troublemaking plans he is hatching, we could find our beloved theatre closed!

Everyone is nervous and this morning, during rehearsal time, Burbage gave us all a warning – "Be careful what you say to strangers. One wrong word and we could all find ourselves being jailed in the Tower of London."

He mimed a nasty neck chop that brought to mind the executed traitors' heads that are displayed on London Bridge, slowly rotting in the wind and rain for all to see. I stole a glance at Mr Shakespeare. He, more than all of us, is in the most danger because of his links with Essex. He stood silently, with no expression on his face. He is a friendly man, but a mysterious man, our playwright.

The Globe Theatre, London

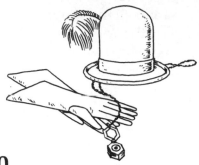

15 October 1600

We are keeping our heads down and working hard. In the mornings we rehearse an old play of Will Shakespeare's, *The Merry Wives of Windsor*, and in the afternoons we are doing a dreary history play called *A Larum for London*. This is not by Mr Shakespeare, and it shows! Although we put on plays by other writers he is definitely the best around. But I am playing only supporting parts, as per usual.

That reminds me. You have never been to London, have you? Well, the life blood of the place is the mighty muddy River Thames. On its north bank is the City of London, surrounded by city walls and home to a great press of people. A bunch of puffed-up merchants have got a stranglehold on City laws and think that the public theatre is a wicked waste of time (and that actors are worse than beggars). These gentlemen generally ban theatre within the City's walls, but you can escape their

16

miserable rules by walking across London Bridge or paying a penny to catch a ferry across to Bankside – that's the name of the street that runs by the southern riverbank. Here you will find all manner of entertainment, including our very own Globe Theatre. If you walked much further from the river you would soon reach muddy fields and get your shoes dirty. On the way you might notice Mr Heminges's higgledy-piggledy thatched house, crammed alongside several others in a narrow street. You might see Mr Heminges's wife on her way out to buy some bread, and remark on her kind face. If you glanced to the top of the building you might see me in my attic window, quill pen in hand.

17 October 1600

Today is Sunday, which means no plays and a welcome day off. I am sitting up in my attic room, which I share with Matthew, another boy apprentice of Mr Heminges and my good friend. It is warm and cosy, with two stools, a couple of candle holders and two straw mattresses (Matthew has been lying on his all day so far).

I write my diary resting on a big old wooden chest filled with various theatre costumes that belong to Mr Heminges. We have a fireplace, and some rushes strewn on the floor. They are swept up and replaced every now and again when they get really dirty. The only bad part of our cosy rooftop home is that we often hear the rats

The City of
London

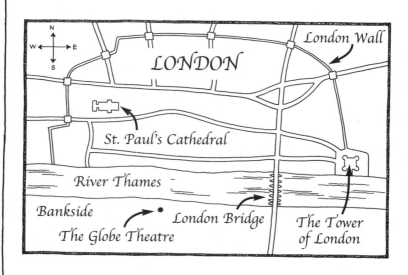

N
W ← → E
S

LONDON

London Wall

St. Paul's Cathedral

River Thames

Bankside

The Globe Theatre

London Bridge

The Tower
of London

circa 1600

scrabbling around in the thatch above.

I have been tiring Matthew by moaning about my theatre parts again. In return he makes friendly but unhelpful suggestions: "The trouble is you look such a baby, and you are too short. Maybe you could stand on a box underneath your skirts. If you didn't move around the stage no one would notice."

Why didn't I think of that before? I'll make sure I always play a statue! But seriously, you don't know any magic ways of getting taller, do you?

20 OCTOBER 1600

I have thought of a way to make everyone think I am more grown-up. I will get a sweetheart and have her visit me at the theatre! I hadn't thought of the idea until this morning when a letter arrived during rehearsal. It was handed to one of the stage hands, who handed it to Matthew, who passed it on to me, saying, "The name 'Will' is written on the front. It must be for you. Go on, read it!"

He and I slipped upstairs to the privacy of the Lords' Room, a private gallery up behind the stage where the grandest members of the audience can avoid the crowd. I untied the ribbon round the note, unfolded it and read:

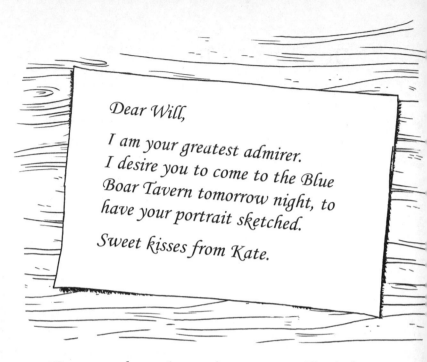

Dear Will,

I am your greatest admirer. I desire you to come to the Blue Boar Tavern tomorrow night, to have your portrait sketched.

Sweet kisses from Kate.

"Someone has taken a fancy to you!" cried Matthew. "Be quiet!" I snapped loudly.

"Hey, you boys up there!" Mr Heminges shouted from the stage below. "Get down here and work. You both need to practise your dance steps."

As I was practising, I mulled the message over in my mind. A portrait! Only the rich and famous have their portraits done. Who could my sweet admirer be? As young as me, surely, or she would not write to me? She must also be rich to afford a painter. I shall go to meet her! With a wealthy sweetheart and a painter doing my portrait I shan't be so easy for people to ignore!

22 October 1600

I have promised to give a full account of my life, warts and all, and not hide anything. Therefore I must tell you how stupid I was last night, as blank and brainless as the full moon that lit my way to the Blue Boar Tavern. I was in my best breeches, doublet and a smart feathered hat secretly borrowed from Mr Heminges's costume chest in our room. I had even rubbed honey on my teeth to freshen them up. I began to wish I hadn't taken all this trouble, for though I knew roughly where the tavern was, I didn't realise I was going to have to walk through such rundown alleys to get there.

I found myself in a tumbledown area that smelt disgustingly of dead dogs.

"'Ere you, all dressed up in yer finery," a woman screeched from a doorway. "What you doin' round 'ere? Do you want a good time? Only a penny." I don't know about a good time, but she'd likely have given me the pox. I reached the tavern with relief. It was large, with a warren of galleries and rooms set around a courtyard – the sort of place where plays were performed in years gone by, before there were many theatres.

"Oh yes. You're expected," said the landlord when I inquired if there was a message for Will. He looked at me a little strangely, then led me up some stairs to a gallery corridor with several doors leading off it. He opened the very last doorway.

"The lady will be here by and by. In the meantime there's some artist fellow waitin' for you."

Inside the wooden-panelled room a tall thin man stood closely up against a wall, almost as if he were listening for something. When I arrived he stepped quickly away from the wall and sat in a chair, his sketching things set out before him. He nodded at me.

"Sit over there, if you please." He waved me to another chair by the wall. "I'm to begin the sketch before the lady returns."

"Have you seen her? Is she pretty?" I asked eagerly. He said nothing, but raised an eyebrow and looked amused. As he sketched and I sat quietly, I noticed the voices of men coming through the wall from the room next door.

"Sounds like a meeting," I remarked, and the artist looked up at me keenly. He seemed about to speak, but at that moment the landlord returned with a tray.

"What's this?" I asked, surprised. There was food laid out on the tray – sugar dough in love-knot shapes, tomatoes, sprigs of mint…

"Aphrodisiac food. Food to put people in the mood for romance," leered the landlord. "Dame Katherine sent them. She'll be here directly when she's finished serving ale to customers." He chuckled and I felt a violent nervous cramp in my stomach. Surely the word 'Dame' meant an older lady, not the sweet young girl I had hoped for. Serving ale? Rich women didn't do that!

The artist interrupted my panicky thoughts. "Don't look so nervous. You're shaking like the jelly I ate last night at the Queen's banquet." The Queen's banquet? Whatever was he doing there? Surely he wasn't from court? What he said next really shocked me: "I must say, I expected the famous William Shakespeare to look, well, a little more mature."

William Shakespeare? Oh, Lord! The truth suddenly dawned on me. The note wasn't for me after all! It was for Mr Shakespeare, yet here I was with a trayful of love biscuits and some kind of grand court artist working away at my sketch! I did what any daft mushy-apple-headed boy would do. I ran for it, blundering out into the corridor. A middle-aged woman was coming the other way, wiping her hands on an apron and muttering: "William, I'm coming! It's your lovely Dame Katherine!"

I bolted in the other direction but found a dead end. I was trapped. So I threw open the door next to the artist's room and jumped inside. A group of men were hunched around a table, talking and jabbing fingers in the air. A phrase floated out of the huddle. "Watch out for the Queen's agents…"

Then the noise of the door slamming shut behind me alerted them to the stranger now standing in their room. They looked up, surprise and suspicion on their faces. A gaunt man was the first to move towards me, his eyes narrowed in anger, and I saw with alarm that a purple scar like a crack ran across his cheek, and there was a gleaming dagger in his belt. What would be worse: Dame Katherine, old enough to be my mother; or a man with a well-tended dagger? Neither would do. I heard the lovestruck lady opening the door to the artist's room. So I turned, quickly rushed out of the door, along the corridor and down the stairs, but heavy footsteps followed me. There was a shout: "Stop him!" But my pursuer was delayed by the landlord getting in the way, and I gained enough time to make it through the entrance on to the street and run for it. I zigzagged through a maze of alleys and then, thanks to my small size, I was able to squeeze into a dark corner and hide there silently, though shaking violently, until I was sure nobody was following me. I took off my conspicuous hat, cursed myself for not bringing a cloak, and made my way home, severely shaken.

1 November 1600

I have been thinking about the mystery of the men at the Blue Boar, and today I got an important clue about them, though a most unwelcome one.

This afternoon, after the play ended, most of the actors went to the Queen's Head, a tavern near the theatre, and Mr Heminges let Matthew and me go too. As usual it was lively. Some of the actors from a rival theatre company, the Admiral's Men, were there, and generally we get along well. Soon we all began singing:

"Heigh-ho, nobody home
Meat, nor drink, nor money have I none.
Still I will be merry!"

Then a man who had been drinking in a corner got up on a table, threw his tankard at the wall and cried out drunkenly: "For Essex! Rise up for Essex!" He was quickly bundled out and nobody admitted that they knew him. But after

that the friendly hubbub of noise died down,
to be replaced by heads bent in quiet discussion.
   I listened closely as rumours and snippets of
conversation swept past my attentive ears.

"There is plotting to overthrow the Queen's advisors. Essex wants to be in control. He could even force the Queen to name him as her successor." Another man spoke, to my left. "Everyone at court is full of nerves in case something happen soon. I heard the Queen's agents, her best spies, are out hunting for plotters."

It began to fit into place... The men meeting in the room next door to me at the Blue Boar must have been these very same political plotters! I heard them mention the Queen's agents. No wonder they chased me; they thought I had overheard their plans! Though I escaped their clutches they might still be out to find me. But they don't know who I am... I am a stranger to them... They might not even remember my face... Unless they see the portrait sketch of me the artist had started, of course!

3 NOVEMBER 1600

Do you think things could be any blacker? Myself possibly a marked man, a threat to those who plot for Essex? Well, believe me, I have found a way to make it all much much worse, as you shall read.

I worried and worried about it all. What if the tavern plotters decide to find me? They only have to look at the portrait sketch and then keep an eye out for me. Sooner or later I could be found lying face down with a knife in my back!

"Matthew, Matthew," I hissed at my friend straight after the afternoon performance. "You must help me. After all, you have put me in danger of my life!"

"Eh?" cried Matthew.

"You gave me that stupid note and it was for William Shakespeare, not me."

"Hold on! It was you that wanted to have a lady admirer!" retorted Matthew. But there was no time for this debate. I hurried him home, telling him about my plan on the way. "We must get back my picture. Dame Katherine will have it. It's evidence that I was there at the tavern. We must get it back!"

"*We?*" squeaked Matthew.

"Yes, we! You helped get me into this stinking heap of trouble. You must help pull me out!" Matthew thought I was mad but I told him my life was in danger, and in the end that was good enough for him.

"I think you may have gone completely crazy, Will, and if so you will need me even more," he reasoned, and agreed to help me.

We waited for Mr Heminges to go out with his wife, and then we raided his costume chest. When we had finished we were both dressed as women. I was a merchant's wife in lace and a large hat. Matthew dressed simply, as my maid (at least I got the best part this time). We didn't have time to put on lots of finery so it's just as well that no one below high rank is allowed to wear grand clothing anyway.

I think, all in all, we looked pretty much the part.

We walked quickly, with our heads down, and when we reached the Blue Boar we nervously went inside. "Evening," said the landlord, eyeing us quizzically. "We don't get fine ladies here as a rule… " We simpered and shrugged. He raised an eyebrow: "Well, I won't ask questions. I know how to keep my mouth shut."

"We were looking for someone, an artist," I said, slipping a coin into his hand.

"Then you'll be wanting to speak to Dame Katherine," he winked and disappeared through a door. Soon Dame Katherine appeared, her sleeves rolled up and her hands looking sticky.

"Gutting pigeons for pies," she explained,

though we never asked. "You want an artist, do you? What makes you think you'll find one here?"

"I heard from a friend there was one in residence," I ventured.

"A friend?"

"William Shakespeare," Matthew blurted out, and I could have killed him!

"Ooh, do you know William?" cooed the daft woman. I thought quickly.

"That's right. He asked us to come and see if he could borrow his sketch for a day or two. It's the one that was done for his portrait. He left in such a hurry he didn't have time to see it. He says he's sorry he had to go and he'll visit you another time."

"Well, let's see now..." Dame Katherine replied. "There was an artist who hung about the bar awhile, and when I asked him what his business was he offered his services to do a portrait or two, at good rates. I invited William over to have his picture done because I've seen him at the Globe and I'm his biggest admirer. He's lovely! Anyway, William did come here, but I missed him on account of having too much work to do..." She glared in the landlord's direction. "By the time I was free the darling man was gone and the artist soon took himself off too, and took his sketch with him, the cheeky beggar. He hasn't been back since. For all I know, he's fallen in the river."

So, the picture was gone. Good! There was no

remaining evidence of me ever having been at the Blue Boar on the night of the full moon. But just then the door opened behind us and my heart tumbled when I saw the scarred man enter, his dagger once again openly on display in his belt. Luckily my disguise was good enough and he didn't look twice at me.

"Ale!" he barked. "Are the others here?"

"Upstairs in the usual room," replied the landlord. So the plotters were meeting again! My heart turned to ice.

"We'll bid you good night," I said.

"You tell that William Shakespeare to come and see me again," shrieked Dame Katherine, standing right next to the man with the scar. I stood frozen to the spot as she turned to him. "Lovely, Will Shakespeare is. He came to visit only the other night. Night of the full moon. Upstairs in the room next to you, he was. Did you see him?"

The man set down his ale pot and stared at the landlord menacingly. "I saw a damned nosy cur in a hurry, but I thought you said you didn't know who he was…"

The landlord shrugged. "I don't ask people's business," he replied. "What Dame Katherine does is her own affair, when she's not serving ale."

"William Shakespeare…" the scarred man hissed quietly, and it seemed to me that the words dripped with malice.

Ye Gods, what have I done? Have I put Mr

Shakespeare in mortal danger from these frightening men? We crept back to Mr Heminges's house, knowing he would still be out with the others. If he ever discovers what we have been up to we will surely lose our acting apprenticeships. But that's nothing if William Shakespeare loses his life on account of an ass like me!

1 DECEMBER 1600

I have been constantly worried that the scarred man will one day appear at the theatre to threaten Mr Shakespeare or me, or both, but there is nothing I can do.

Matthew thinks I am letting my head run as wild as a runaway horse. "Look at the facts, Will. Firstly, you don't know for certain these plotters for Essex are after you. Secondly, even if they are, they think you are William Shakespeare."

"But that puts him in danger!"

"No, no. You've got it all muddled. Look, they won't mind Will Shakespeare hearing their business, will they? Everyone knows he's on Essex's side. So there. Nothing to worry about... except..."

"What?"

"Oh, nothing."

"Tell me!"

"Well, I was just thinking... It's the Queen's agents you might need to worry about. They're on the lookout for plots against the court, aren't they? If they discover this lot at the Blue Boar, and link Mr Shakespeare to them, then it's the Tower for him. And perhaps no more Globe Theatre. Didn't you say that artist said he was from the Queen's court? What was he doing in that smelly old tavern, do you think?"

So, instead of calming me down, Matthew has now taken away all my sleep and left my brain a buzzing beehive of fears and questions. That artist said he had been at one of the Queen's banquets. Was he a spy? And what is my best course of action? If I try to warn Mr Shakespeare he will learn how I borrowed Mr Heminges's costumes and put him in danger. I would leave here tomorrow in disgrace, my acting career ruined. On the other hand, maybe it will all come to nothing if I just wait. Yes, perhaps nothing will happen and it will all blow over. That's what I'll do. I'll wait...

23 DECEMBER 1600

I was just beginning to believe all was safe when this afternoon I had a scare that made me fearful again. I was sitting backstage in the tiring room, waiting for my scene. Thomas, our tireman, looks after things there, and he was quietly chatting to me. "From what I hear the Queen will be getting treason for Christmas! Her agents will nip it all in the bud, though. No doubt she's got all her best spies working on it. They'll keep the executioners busy. What's the matter, Will? You look as if you've seen a headless ghost!"

I went on stage in a fluster and almost forgot my lines. Our stage prompter looked anxiously at me a couple of times, ready to whisper the forgotten words to me from his copy of the play. I remembered them just in time.

25 DECEMBER 1600

We got the day off today because it is the beginning of the twelve days of Christmas, a welcome diversion from spies and plots. The house was decorated with evergreen boughs and branches, and Mrs Heminges cooked us a feast of mutton-filled minced pies, and a hearty potage stew. I helped her to make a pot of wassail just like we used to get given when we went carolling in Marlborough. Do you remember, Judith? The smell made me suddenly homesick – the roast apples mingled with spices in the warm ale… I toasted all of my family back home, especially you, my dear sister, as I drank it down.

30 DECEMBER 1600

Last night we played at the private house of our patron, the Lord Chamberlain, Lord Hunsdon, at Blackfriars. We all like private performances, partly because the company gets paid well and partly because we act indoors. What bliss to be warm in a fine wood-panelled hall, while frost makes its patterns outside.

Lord Hunsdon was rather old and creaky-looking, but seemed kind. All theatre companies must have an important patron, by law, but Mr Heminges says we're lucky to have such a decent one, not a rogue who demands a big cut of our takings and does nothing for us. Lord Hunsdon is our protector and champion at court, and in return we perform for him, his family and friends. They were all very elegantly dressed in the latest court fashions. Eventually we may wear some of these clothes on stage, because when they get too dirty the ladies and gentlemen replace them and give the old outfits to their servants, who in their turn sell them on to Mr Burbage. With a bit of freshening up, they do nicely as costumes.

When our play was over we lesser players were invited down to the kitchens, where hot wine and pies were ready for us. Meanwhile, the sharers stayed upstairs with Lord Hunsdon to talk and eat grander fare – salted beef, rabbit stew and roasted game birds.

It was warm and wonderful in the kitchens. Fires glowed underneath pots and spits and the

smell of baking wafted out from the brick ovens. I fell into conversation with the kitchen boys who told me some interesting court news. See how tittle-tattle spreads from the lords and ladies in the grandest hall down to the lowest pot stirrer?

They saw Queen Elizabeth at Lord Hunsdon's house in the autumn, and say she is beginning to show her sixty-seven years. Though she covers her face with an ever-thicker paste of white lead and vinegar, she cannot hide the sharpness of her old bones. According to gossip she makes her health worse by taking a bath every month, when everyone knows that any more than two a year just isn't safe.

"She shouldn't use that white lead make-up," I said, joining in the gossip. "It makes the skin all grey and shrivelled. On stage, we use a paste of boiled egg white or alum. It costs a lot less and it doesn't ruin your skin."

"Well, lad. You tell her next time you see her!" A fat greasy-faced cook clapped me hard on the back. "She won't notice you, though. She's got a handsome guest and she can't take her eyes off him! The Queen of France has sent her a dashing messenger, an Italian by the name of Orsino, Duke of Bracchiano. He dances with her and pays her compliments as if she were young again. She loves it, does our good Queen Bess!"

31 DECEMBER 1600

This morning Mr Heminges told us something of what was said at Lord Hunsdon's table. I was all ears, as you can imagine, desperate to hear what the coming months might hold for us all.

Mr Heminges began: "Our patron is worried about the situation with the Earl of Essex, whose banishment from court has made his temper reach boiling point. Lord Hunsdon says that as long as the theatre company keeps well away from any involvement with the Earl of Essex's schemes he should be able to ensure we'll be left alone. Lord Hunsdon has confirmed that the Queen has sent agents out to spy on those who make plots to help the Earl of Essex. So, all of you, keep your heads down." As he turned away he muttered under his breath, "I just hope Will Shakespeare has the wit to keep well away from danger…"

Oh dear! It may be too late for hoping! Now I really am afraid about what may be coming…

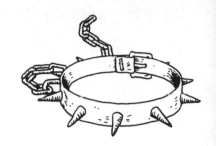

4 January 1601

I write this feeling feverish and hot, even though it is frozen outside. It is the middle of the day, but I am not going to the theatre this afternoon. Instead Mrs Heminges has put me to bed with a hot drink of mint and ginger. Illness may stop me writing soon but while I can I will try to tell my story.

Recently I seem to have been on stage for every waking hour. Mr Heminges said I should work and rehearse, work and rehearse, always putting myself before Mr Burbage's eyes, if I wanted to be considered for the best female parts.

I was performing yesterday, just finishing my lines, when Thomas the tireman's arm snaked out from the door at the back of the stage and pulled me back through it, much to the amusement of the groundlings in the audience. "He's not that bad!" one of them cried. The other actors carried on professionally, pretending nothing had happened, while Thomas spoke to me urgently backstage.

"Look, there's a gentleman out the back waiting to speak to you, Will. He's very well dressed and I'd say he was some sort of court official if I had to guess his part. Characters like that don't bring good news as a rule, so I thought I'd warn you now."

I hurried to rip off my costume. "Watch out! That's expensive stuff, that is!" cried Thomas. I gave up, unable to undo all the fastenings, but I smeared the make-up off my face as best I could, threw my wig into a corner and grabbed a long-hooded cloak meant for the part of some king or other.

"Hold on, Will! Hold on!" cried Thomas, but I ran, down the back stairs and out of a side door past the startled doorman. I believed, and still do, that my mystery visitor was a Queen's agent come to take me to the Tower of London and make me tell all I knew about the Essex plotters and about Shakespeare. I've heard they torture people in the Tower to obtain confessions. Perhaps they would put me on a rack and stretch my limbs until I confessed anything that came into my head!

I ran blindly through the dirty street, never daring to look back, turning this way and that to lose any pursuer, until I reached a dead end and hopped over a low curved wall into a bear-baiting pit. On bear-baiting days crowds line the walls, cheering, but today it was empty. I ran on, out of the ring into a courtyard beyond, where a deep growl stopped me dead in my tracks. I had stumbled into an area ringed with dog kennels, and though they were tied up, a couple of huge mastiff dogs were stirring at my approach. They began to bark crazily, their massive heads bigger than a grown man's and their teeth the stuff of nightmares. Though they normally attack a chained bear in the pit, it seemed I would do just as well, and the thought almost engulfed me in terror.

"Shut up! Shut up!" I muttered to the dogs. Their noise could raise the alarm and lead my enemy to me. Was that spy even now close on my trail? I dived through a side door into a long barn-sized room strewn with stinking hay. Though the dogs could still smell my scent they no longer saw me moving, and at last they lost interest and quietened down, thanks be to God. I ventured further into the barn's shadows, and froze, eye to eye with a bear.

He was in a corner cage, his wide shoulders hunched, a thick spiked collar round his neck fixed by a brutal chain. He did not stir but sat still, empty with despair. Tomorrow, I thought... Tomorrow I could be in the Tower, chained up like you, ready to lie and betray to spare myself more pain. I shivered, wrapped my cloak around me and prepared to spend a night in hiding.

Early next morning I heard a commotion and peered out from my hiding place in the bear's barn. Out in the courtyard two evil-looking dogs were being held on their leads by a man. A horse stood tethered to a post, its eyes rolling in terror.

Suddenly, the man spoke. "Training time, beauties. You'll find this old nag less trouble than a bear. Still, killing is killing, and practice makes perfect." The man hissed and let the dogs go. They ran at the trapped horse and what followed was a sickening sight, though by God's mercy the poor horse died swiftly.

When the dogs had done their work, the man led them back into their kennels, and returned outside just as I emerged from my hiding place. Our eyes met for a moment before I ran for my life. I don't know what he thought, seeing a boy with his face half smeared with white make-up, hitching up his skirts as he ran from the bear's barn. He said nothing, gave no sign that he knew who I was. But I knew him. He had a scar on his cheek more livid than ever in the morning sunlight. I didn't dare to look back to see if he followed, in case a glance slowed me down or filled me with too much fear to move.

I did my best, running through the Bankside alleys. Thank Heaven it was still early morning and most people were still abed, for I made a sorry sight. But I could not run forever, weak as I was with hunger and cold. Eventually I had to stop, panting and doubled over. The cold winter air stung my lungs. I stayed hidden in a doorway until I was sure there was no sign of the scarred man pursuing me. Then I used back ways to get down to the river, half thinking to find a boat and escape from all damnable Queen's agents and bear-pit villains. The quay was empty, so I sat wretchedly by the boat steps leading into the black Thames water. Who knows where I would be now if Matthew had not found me?

"Will! Thank goodness! We've all been out looking for you. Why did you run away like that?"

"A Queen's agent came for me," I replied, still dazed and afraid.

"Don't fear so much, Will. He went away again, it seems, after talking privately with Mr Burbage. Perhaps all is not so ill. Come on. I'll take you home."

I followed meekly, hardly able to think any more. Mrs Heminges took one look at me and said I was plainly very ill. I was bundled straight up here to my room. Matthew has moved his things out and Mrs Heminges has given strict orders for me not to be disturbed.

To tell the truth I ache all over, and must put down the diary. Please forgive me, Judith. May God and Mr Shakespeare forgive me, too!

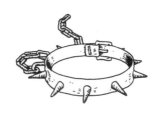

10 FEBRUARY 1601

Dearest Judith, I have failed again in my aim of giving you a full account of life here in London, for I have been ill with a fever and have been unable to write in my diary until today. Some recent days are complete blanks in my memory. I vaguely remember others when I seem to have been in a world of dreams, with imaginary visitors at my bedside – the artist who sketched me at the Blue Boar, Mr Burbage – even a dream figure of our old Uncle Silas, for some reason. Mrs Heminges has brought me round though, dosing me with powders and potions, and now I am feeling a little better. She will not let me get up yet and says I must rest.

11 FEBRUARY 1601

Mrs Heminges allowed Matthew to come and sit with me today, it being Sunday and his day off from the theatre. He has told me that you know about my illness and has read me your letter and Father's, both of which I will place in this diary.

14 January 1601   Marlborough

Dearest Will,

We have worrying news of you from Uncle Silas.
He came up to London on business and visited the
Globe to see you play. He was told you were ill and
went to Mr Heminges's house, where you were
poorly with a fever. He saw you but says you did
not recognise him. He says you do not have any of
the boils or sores that the plague would bring, but
even so we are all very worried for you.

He is to go back to London in the next few days
to finish his business, and will bring this letter for
you to read when you are well enough, and lots of
medicine made up by Father, together with his
instructions for Mrs Heminges. Father says you
must rest. So make sure you do so, for the sake of
all who care for you, and by God's mercy you will
get well once again.

My fondest love,   Judith

PS: Mr Morton, your old schoolmaster, sends his
good wishes. He says his current class of boys are
like a horde of clumsy puppies. I told him he should
teach girls instead. He looked shocked to his very
bones at the thought! He said the day women went
to school would be the day that Hell froze over,
and I was a very odd girl even to think of it. I
hope this makes you smile.

To Mistress Heminges,

Instructions for the care of my son, William Savage.

I have been told my son Will is ill with a fever, and that you are taking the greatest care of him. I am much indebted to you for your gentle kindness to him. But I beg you, on no account send for any local barber, the sort who says they practise medicine. In my opinion most of them are incompetent or worse! A barber would probably want to let out some of Will's blood but I prefer not to have cuts made in my son, as I have often seen these make a patient worse.

I have knowledge of medicine and I am therefore sending my own mixture of powdered herbs and roots that have powers of healing. I have included liquorice and comfrey to ease his chest and feverfew to lessen the heat of his brow. There is also some valerian to calm him. When he is on the mend be sure to give him a warm drink made from the leaves of the lemon balm I have sent, and some almonds steeped in milk which will help return his strength to him.

God bless you for the care of my son, who is most dear to me.

Samuel Savage
Apothecary

12 FEBRUARY 1601

Your kind words have made me feel a hundred
times better, Judith, and, according to Matthew,
Father's practical help has saved me from the
local barber, who pretends to know medicine as
well as shaving, but is a butcher by all accounts
and loses more patients than he saves. Matthew
sat with me again today and told me the tale of
all I have missed – it turns out a great deal.

He says trouble began a week ago, when a
group of men arrived at the Globe Theatre
during rehearsal. When Burbage saw them, he
dismissed the hired players and boys but asked
the sharers to stay. Being very curious, Matthew
slipped under the stage and hid in the space
beneath. One of the visitors introduced himself.

"Lord Meyrick, at your service."

"I know your face," replied Burbage. "I have
seen you watching the plays from the Lords'
Room, have I not?'

"Yes, and I know that your company are strong
and steadfast supporters of my lord, the Earl of
Essex. He wishes you to perform Mr Shakespeare's
play, *Richard the Second*, on the night of the seventh
of February. He will pay you well for it."

"*Richard the Second*? That's an old play. We
won't get much audience for it," parried
Burbage. "Besides, my players won't have time
to rehearse it."

"An old play yes, but a significant one. It
concerns the fate of a monarch who trusted too
well in bad advisors. It will send a clear message

to the Queen that her citizens will not tolerate those who advise her any longer since they have poisoned her mind against such a well-loved and loyal gentleman as Essex."

"It is asking for trouble…" some of the sharers murmured unhappily.

Lord Meyrick then turned to Mr Shakespeare and spoke to him directly. "The Earl of Southampton is the strongest supporter Essex has, and I believe he is your old friend, who has lent you his patronage and goodwill many a time. He asks you to do this as a personal favour."

"Then it must be done." Mr Shakespeare spoke quietly and no one argued further until Lord Meyrick and his men had left. Some said anxiously that the play would be certain to upset the Queen, but Will Shakespeare was not to be moved.

"The Earl of Southampton is my friend and the Earl of Essex is my old patron. Without their generous support I would never have made it this far in the theatre. I owe them my career and must repay the debt. If you will not do this with me I must go and read the play myself.

Then Mr Burbage addressed all the sharers: "Shakespeare is our friend and our playwright. We stick together, good or bad. That's how we players do things. Besides, this is a gamble that we may just win."

Then Shakespeare addressed everyone there. "If any of you are in doubt, I will understand you not taking part…"

Nobody refused. That's how players are, Judith. We stick together; look out for each other. As Mr Heminges said afterwards: "Whichever way God writes the play, we players must stand together."

13 FEBRUARY 1601

I have heard more of Matthew's story, and it is very worrying. On the night of the seventh of February, the Chamberlain's Men played *Richard the Second* as asked. Matthew says the theatre crowd were very different from the usual happy buzzing crew of law students, merchant families and wise-cracking young gentlemen. Instead they were serious-faced Essex supporters who listened hard and cheered at any lines that spoke of bad royal advisors. Matthew says the players stumbled a bit over unfamiliar lines, and the prompter had more to do than usual, but the crowd didn't seem to notice. The play was stirring up popular feeling for the Earl of Essex as Lord Meyrick must have intended.

Everyone there that night must have felt certain of success. They were going to march into the City of London the very next day and they were sure all the ordinary citizens would join with them in rebellion, such was the popularity of the Earl of Essex. They thought that an ever-growing mob of thousands would surround the Queen's palace and force her to imprison her hated new advisors and return Essex to court, whether she liked it or not. With Essex back in a powerful position, the Globe Theatre would be quite safe from closure. Perhaps that was what Burbage

meant when he said we might win the gamble of performing *Richard the Second*.

But this audience had misread the plot. Outside in the real world a cold wind blew down empty city streets the next day when the Earl of Essex rode in through the city gate, splendidly dressed, with his deluded supporters behind him – too small a crowd to scare a Queen. It was a rebellion that never took hold and it soon petered out like a dying fire. No one came out to join them. No one was prepared to rebel against the Queen's orders. So Essex had to admit defeat and returned to his house a beaten man. Later he was arrested, along with his supporters, and locked in the Tower of London.

14 FEBRUARY 1601

At the end of Matthew's story I was very anxious. What will happen to the Globe and to Shakespeare? Mr Heminges himself came upstairs and sat with me to answer my questions. I asked him what had been happening and he replied, "The Queen's agents have been rounding up rebels, but they haven't come for Mr Shakespeare, so that's a good sign. I believe he has worked out his own way of winning back favour with Her Majesty. We'll see in time if it works. Meanwhile, our patron, Lord Hunsdon, will try to convince the Queen that we were given no choice but to play *Richard the Second*. But things are in the balance, Will, I can't pretend otherwise. We do know that the Earl of Essex is to be executed on the twenty-fifth of February. He's a doomed man. I hope we are not!"

16 FEBRUARY 1601

I am up at last, feeling much better. There is extraordinary news, though, Judith. The Chamberlain's Men have been summoned to court to play there for the Queen on the twenty-fourth of February, the very night before the Earl of Essex is executed! What can it mean? Will the Queen damn us there and then? Perhaps it will be our last ever performance!

Though I am not yet strong enough to take a stage part, I am to help the company's musicians. We are doing a new play by Mr Shakespeare called *Twelfth Night*, and there is lots of music in it. Mr Heminges says we are not to worry ourselves about what will happen, as there is nothing we can do. We must trust to God and Will Shakespeare's talent as a playwright to pull us through this crisis.

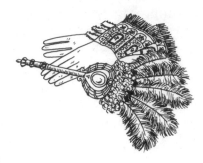

1 MARCH 1601

You will, I am sure, be keen to know what occurred during the play at court (at the Queen's Palace of Whitehall) on the twenty-fourth of February. As you know, I was to help the musicians by playing a pipe (an actor has to be multi-talented to last around here). To do this I sat by the stage, and was able to get a really good view of all the goings on in the Great Hall where we set up our stage. To begin with everyone in the company was very nervous. Even Mr Burbage was muttering, "I hope this works. She's unpredictable." I think he meant the Queen. The audience were glittering. Fine jewels and pearls studded both their clothes and their hair. I saw our patron, Lord Hunsdon, sitting near the front.

"It's tense here at court tonight," remarked Mr Heminges quietly to me before the show. "These people all knew the Earl of Essex well. Some have been friends with him for years. Tomorrow he will be dead, and it's bound to be on their minds. I hope Lord Hunsdon has done the trick and persuaded Her Majesty not to close the Globe Theatre for good."

"What about Mr Shakespeare? Is he safe?" I asked anxiously.

"We shall see; we shall see," he mused.

When the Queen entered the room there was a hush. She was bedecked in finery – a dress with a tall, stiff lace collar, heavily embroidered sleeves, wide skirts and bodice, so encrusted with silver thread and pearls that she seemed to shimmer like moonlight. She used her clothes and make-up to good effect, but we players are used to the tricks of theatrical disguise. I could tell that beneath her skirt frame and her stiff bodicing she was a small thin figure and she was getting old.

She sat stiffly, her lips thin but painted scarlet to stand out vividly from her white, white face. The corners of this small but startling mouth were turned down.

The play began with a speech by the main male character:

"If music be the food of love, play on,
Give me excess of it."

I believe the Queen almost began to laugh. I swear I saw the merriment in her eyes. Orsino! William Shakespeare had named the main male character Orsino, after her beloved Italian count, the handsome man I had heard of in Lord Hunsdon's kitchen; the one who danced with her and seemed to melt the weight of her years away.

He was no longer at court, but Mr Shakespeare had conjured up pleasant thoughts of him in the Queen's mind.

The rest of the play was magical, both gentle and full of enchantment. It ran upon disguise, misunderstanding and confusion, then finally understanding brought about by true love. It was designed perfectly to transport the mind away from the awful realities of treason, death and age and to remind it instead of youth and romance. The Queen's face began to soften as she watched, and the years seemed to drop away from her. William Shakespeare is a clever man. I believe he used his greatest skill, that of writing, to save himself that night.

When the play had ended the Queen sat for a while, smiling. When she smiled she looked beautiful. She waved her hand and motioned to Lord Hunsdon to help her up.

"I think we're forgiven," whispered Matthew when I saw him backstage. "That was probably the best night's work we've ever done!"

The night wasn't over for me, though. Mr Burbage tapped me on the shoulder. "Put away your music, Will. There's someone who wants to see you."

He led me down a dark corridor heavy with tapestries. At last he pulled one aside to reveal a doorway, and you can imagine my shock when I saw none other than the artist from the

Blue Boar, holding up the portrait sketch he had done of me! He spoke to me in a calm but firm voice.

"Will, I am glad to see you are well again. The last time I visited you, you were too ill to recognise me or Mr Burbage here."

I looked from one to the other, confused, as Mr Burbage introduced us.

"Will, this is Sir John Crosse, and he has told me about your visits to the Blue Boar."

I assumed at that moment that I was finished for good.

"Sit down, Will. I can see confusion in your face," Sir John Crosse said, smiling. "Mr Burbage knows all, and has co-operated most helpfully, which went a long way to saving his theatre company in this tricky time. Let me explain."

"I was at the Blue Boar on the Queen's business. I am a Queen's agent, you see, and I was investigating there. I hung about the place in the guise of an artist. The barmaid Dame Katherine's obsession with Mr Shakespeare was very helpful to me there because it gave me an excuse to stay. I was surprised to meet you, not him, and even more surprised when you ran away like you did! The landlord at the inn is a friend of mine. He told me how you came back in a very good disguise and no one spotted your true identity but him."

"Good acting, Will!" added Mr Burbage.

"But why?" I asked, my brain more fogged than ever. Sir John leant towards me. "We had reason to believe a gang was plotting at the inn, and we wanted to know their business. I chose that room I was in very carefully, so that I could overhear some of their plans."

"So they were plotting for Essex! I knew it!" I blurted out. "I am not involved, and nor was Mr Shakespeare. Please believe me!"

"Calm down, Will! You'll make yourself ill again!" interrupted Burbage. "Will Shakespeare is safe enough, especially after tonight when he has won his way back into the Queen's favour, but in any event I have suggested it would be better for him to go home to Stratford until everything has blown over."

Sir John stood up and paced around the room as he continued. "You see, Will, the gang weren't exactly plotting for the Earl of Essex, though they hoped to profit from his attempted rebellion. In fact, they are common villains. They work together to rob, cheat, perhaps even to murder for gain. Believe me, the Queen's agents are as interested in destroying all villains who threaten the peace of Her Majesty's realm, whether they be cutthroats or rebels. Our job is to protect the Queen from danger, but also her subjects."

"I heard them say Essex's name!" I cried.

"They knew of the intended rebellion, certainly, and they were working a plan around it. They intended to follow the Earl into the City, mingling with his real supporters. Then they would loot and steal freely as mayhem broke out. Of course, Londoners did not rally to Essex's side as he hoped they would."

He stole a glance at Burbage, who smiled at me and spoke. "Sir John visited the theatre to find you, Will. You, of course, did your own disappearing act!" He raised his eyebrows. "But meeting Sir John gave me the chance to offer him some help in future, which I think may have helped convince some important people that we are not disloyal."

"What sort of co-operation?" I asked.

"Costumes, advice, acting talent… In fact, I hope you will lend your obvious acting talent to the plan, Will. That talent has been amply proved by your adventures in disguise at the Blue Boar! Mr Heminges and I have both agreed that Sir John can ask you, but you must have the final say."

"Will you agree to use your theatrical talent to help me catch the criminals?" Sir John pointed a finger directly at me…

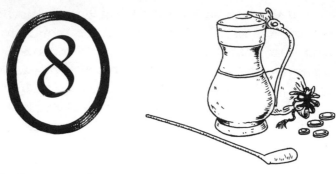

15 APRIL 1601

Will Shakespeare is still away in Stratford,
keeping out of the way until the memory of
the Earl of Essex's rebellion is less fresh in
powerful minds. Meanwhile we are doing a
tedious play called *Satiromastix*. We all hope
Mr Shakespeare is using his time away to write
a new play for us because we sorely need his
magic touch. The crowds at the Globe are thin,
and Mr Heminges, who does the theatre
accounts, has been tutting over the lack of
pennies in the entrance boxes. What we need is
a sparkling new play by our best playwright,
with a fine story that will get them queuing to
come across the Thames and see it.

Meanwhile I have another, more curious
acting role, which I must undertake tomorrow
night on behalf of Sir John Crosse. I am to go
back to the Blue Boar where a meeting of the
criminals is apparently planned. This time I will
be disguised as a maid, and if I play the part well
the landlord will be the only person aware of my

real identity. I will serve the gang their ale and listen to their plans. If something goes wrong the landlord cannot help me either, as he must remain unsuspected. If I am unmasked as a spy, and if this diary is ended here, commend my soul to God. For I shall be dead with a dagger in my ribs.

17 APRIL 1601

I am back! My quill hasn't gone silent after all. I am feeling excited because I think I put in a bravura performance last night at the Blue Boar, though no one applauded me. No, you are the only audience for my story, so perhaps you will give me a quiet cheer when you have read it.

Mr Heminges had to be told of the plan, of course, as I was his apprentice. Matthew had to be told as well, because he would be bound to notice my comings and goings. He was sworn to secrecy.

Mr Burbage himself helped to get me ready in the disguise of a maid. This time, he said, my shortness and my young-looking face would be a great asset to the part. I wore simple plain-coloured skirts, a bodice over a smock, and plain leather slippers – not at all grand. I wore a mouse-coloured wig and a cap to keep it back off my face. There was no fan to manage, no elaborate curtseying or hand gestures. I was to play a real person, simply and naturally, a performance on which I knew my life depended.

Mr Burbage knows just how to give an actor confidence.

"You are perfectly trained for this, Will. It's what you do every day at the Globe – not just imitating women but enchanting an audience into believing in their hearts that you are a woman, when in their minds they know you are not. You do it regularly, and you do it brilliantly. Remember that."

I had little make-up on, just a smudge of red on my cheeks as a barmaid might use. I pulled a few strands of hair out of place to make myself look slightly untidy, and set off for the tavern early in the afternoon, having been excused the play. (Mr Burbage told everyone I was unwell.) When I arrived at the Blue Boar, the landlord introduced me as Mary, a new member of staff, to Dame Katherine who was cleaning up the place. She leant on her broom and looked me up and down sourly.

"The landlord here says you come recommended, though by whom he seems to have forgotten. There isn't much of you, is there? Lets hope you can stomach hard work. We'll be doubly busy tonight."

She thrust the broom towards me. "Get sweeping then. These old floor rushes need chuckin' out."

If I didn't look dishevelled and overworked before, I did by the end of the afternoon and a few hours of floor-sweeping later! My hair was full of dust and my clothes grimier than ever.

When I had at last finished sweeping, the landlord showed me where to find the tankards and ale barrels. "Right, little 'un. We've got a big gathering upstairs tonight. You'll be kept busy serving 'em."

There was a tricky moment when Dame Katherine raised her bushy eyebrows.

"Do you think that's wise?" she asked. "They're very particular, that lot. If she gets anything wrong you'll soon know about it by their anger."

The landlord deftly saved the day by replying sharply to her: "Don't fret, woman! You can see she knows what she's about. This little chit was born to the innkeeping trade," he replied, and immediately gave the old crone several jobs to be getting on with in the kitchen to distract her from criticising me. She gave me a very unfriendly scowl before leaving.

I began to feel more nervous as the evening wore on, and men began to arrive and go upstairs to the meeting room. They called for ale, plenty of it, and I was sent up with tankards and flagons. No one glanced at me and I took care to stay unobtrusive, well away from centre stage, you might say. But it took all my courage not to cry out when the door swung open and in walked the man with the scar on his cheek. I left the room as swiftly as I could, seemingly to get more ale, but really to try to compose myself.

He had seen me twice before and there was a chance he might recognise me. The time had come for me to act as well as I possibly could.

I walked back into the room carrying another ale flagon and served him over his shoulder as he sat at a table. I kept my eyes down so as not to meet his. You cannot hide the eyes with acting or disguises. He glanced up. Did he half remember an image of a white-faced boy hiding in a barn, or of a more well-dressed one who had blundered into this very room?

Suddenly I couldn't make my limbs obey me, couldn't move from the spot. The landlord saved the scene and in a fine piece of stage movement, he subtly put himself between me and the scarred man.

"Go on, girl. Hurry downstairs." He ordered me about my business and I left, mightily relieved. I kept out of the scarred man's view after that and concentrated on keeping my ears open for any evidence I could relay to Sir John.

My training in remembering lines served me well. I can still recall everything I heard. Being small and plain, I was of no consequence, and they said enough in my presence to make it clear they were trying to think of some new crime that would net them a haul of money and goods.

"Pity Essex didn't stir up trouble on the streets. We'd have got clean away with a fair bit during all the chaos of a more successful rebellion."

"We need something like that again, a big jostling crowd so we can steal from their pockets with no one noticing."

But though I heard a lot it seemed they hadn't yet fixed on a plan, and by the end of the night I knew that I would have to come back soon and play the part of Mary once again.

24 APRIL 1601

Will Shakespeare has returned and we are all excited. He has brought back a new play: well, part of it anyway. He's still writing it, but we are to start rehearsing what he has done straightaway. The most thrilling news is that there is a leading role for me! Today Mr Shakespeare and Mr Burbage called me over.

"Richard tells me your acting is going from strength to strength, Will. Good. I am writing a leading part for you in this new play. I have done with writing comedies for a while. These last few months have changed my mood. So this new one is to be a tragedy, the story of a man who slides towards disaster as surely as the sun slides across the sky. He is a prince named Hamlet, and you shall be his lady love, Ophelia. I have written her with you in mind. She is a young girl and has a look of sweet innocence, but in the end she goes mad, so you will need to act strongly and well."

"Well done! You deserve it, Will," Mr Burbage slapped me on the back, at the same time deftly steering me away from Mr Shakespeare so he could whisper in my ear: "I believe your other part is not yet finished. We must hope it is over soon or you will be sorely stretched. We begin rehearsals for *Hamlet* immediately."

So by day I must rehearse Ophelia. Then, because of my continued "illness" I am excused a part in *Satiromastix*, and I am free to work at the Blue Boar as Mary. I must be there, even when there are no villains meeting, otherwise I will arouse suspicions.

I never knew it was such hard work being a serving wench. Poor Mary! All this hard work is giving her (me) sore feet, and on top of that she must put up with the jealous Dame Katherine, who never misses a chance to criticise her. Her part is one I'd gladly give to someone else, if I had the chance.

4 MAY 1601

We are well into rehearsals for *Hamlet*, so it is a
relief that yesterday I made my last appearance
as Mary, the maid at the Blue Boar. The landlord
told me the criminals would be meeting again
in the room upstairs, and I was to serve them
their ale, as before.

A couple of the gang members arrived early
and had a drink downstairs, where they were
subjected to the charms of Dame Katherine. She
had long made it clear with glances and barbed
remarks that she thought she should go upstairs
to serve such important clients, not me. Now,
given the chance, she wanted to make her mark.

"I am so excited. You'll never guess why!"
she announced girlishly to the early arrivals.
They did not bother to answer.

"There's to be a new play at the Globe
Theatre!" At this point I almost dropped a
flagon in surprise but nobody noticed and she
carried on.

"William Shakespeare, the finest playwright
alive, wrote it. They say it will be his best yet

71

and there are sure to be crowds going. I'm a regular of course. Mr Shakespeare is a close friend. Some very grand people go to the plays, you know. Oh yes. Very finely dressed people indeed, with jewels and everything."

At this a weasel-faced man looked up keenly and replied in an oily voice: "Is that so? Well then, it'll be worth going, I dare say." He winked at his companions. "Thank you, lovely lady. I'd like to hear more of your obvious expertise on theatre matters. Will you be serving the ale at our meeting tonight? I hope so." Dame Katherine positively glowed with pleasure, and gave me a look of triumph.

Once again the scarred man arrived to join the gang, and once again I did my best to keep out of his line of sight. It was easier this time because all the attention was on Dame Katherine, whom they had called up to the room. Judging correctly that she had a runaway mouth they proceeded to ask her several questions about the Globe Theatre. She was more than happy to give them every detail she knew of what happened there when a play was performed.

When she had gone back downstairs I followed her out of the room, but lingered outside the door as I left and heard the voices of the gang.

"It's a sitting duck, lads. I say we visit on the opening night of this new play. Some of us can pick the pockets of the audience during the performance. Plus there are the theatre takings to steal."

"It'll be a decent enough haul. Not what we were expecting to make from robbing the crowds during Essex's rebellion, but not bad."

"We'll do it." I recognised the voice of the scarred man. "Picking the pockets of the crowd will be simple enough and the takings boxes can be easily stolen from the doormen while the play is on. Show their throats a sharp knife!"

He was a chilling creature.

I left the Blue Boar forever after that night, having gained the information I needed. To avert suspicion the landlord agreed to tell everyone he had fired me for being a good-for-nothing lazy slattern. The next day I told Mr Burbage what I had heard so he could get word to Sir John.

"You did well," Burbage told me. "But now your part in this is finished. It's up to Sir John to catch the thieves. Now keep your mind on acting Ophelia and leave the rest to others, Will." I felt very relieved to have the weight taken off my shoulders, but I have one regret. Judith, I wish you had seen me playing Mary! I think you would have laughed and tut-tutted at my grubby skirts and dusty hair.

7 MAY 1601

Hamlet rehearsals are in full swing, and when I asked Mr Burbage about Sir John's plans he told me that things are being sorted out. "Keep your mind on acting." My character, Ophelia, goes mad and finally the audience hears that she has drowned. So I must practise my mad scenes. There are some standard stage gestures used to convey madness but Mr Heminges has told me not to rely on them. "Make Ophelia natural. She will seem all the more sad."

I have to sing a bawdy song which is very rude, but must sing it in such a way that the effect is tragic, because it is obvious my character is losing her mind. At first I wear the costume of a noblewoman, with a smock, stockings, fine petticoats and skirts, bodice, lace collar and, of course, a bum-roll, to give me a more female shape at the back. But when Ophelia goes mad I wipe off as much make-up as I can and appear dressed only in the smock, as if I had become too crazy to change out of my nightgown.

In this play Mr Burbage has the starring role of Hamlet, Prince of Denmark. Mr Armin, the company's best comic actor, is a joking gravedigger. Shakespeare himself has a small part, playing the ghost of Hamlet's murdered father. At one point he booms out his lines from a hiding place under the stage. Mostly he is busy watching the rest of us, making suggestions and changing lines here and there.

"Keep your swords up, gentlemen. Try fighting round the stage pillars."

"Matthew, come over to the left. We can't see you behind the soldiers."

Matthew is playing Hamlet's mother, Gertrude, and Mr Heminges plays Hamlet's stepfather, Claudius, whom Hamlet thinks has murdered his father. Other sharers have taken smaller parts, and there are a few hired actors who play guards and servants.

Judith, I think Mr Shakespeare must have been thinking about death while he was writing *Hamlet*, perhaps because Essex so lately met

Fan wig

Farthingale

Lace collar

Bodice

Stockings

Garters to
hold up
stockings

Leather shoes

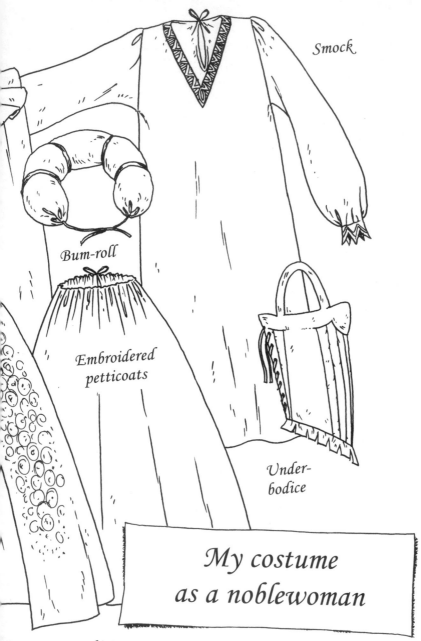

Smock

Bum-roll

Embroidered
petticoats

Under-
bodice

My costume
as a noblewoman

Topmost skirt

with the executioner's axe. Thomas has had to dig around in his prop store and dust down an old skull needed for one scene. "One skull, for use by Hamlet," he announced cheerfully when he found it. "'Tis said that this particular one belonged to an old actor who was determined that death wouldn't stop him being a success on the stage. Nice of Mr Shakespeare to write him a part."

There's a lot of sword fighting in the play. Someone even gets accidentally stabbed while hiding behind the cloth hangings at the back of the stage. Oh, and in one scene there is even an acting company performing a play for Hamlet! All in all, it is sure to be a great success, I think. The first night is approaching fast!

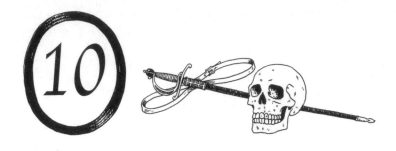

10 May 1601

It is night, and raining softly outside the bedroom window, a spring shower that has released damp smells of wood and thatch from the house. I cannot sleep. Tomorrow is the first performance of *Hamlet* and, though I have been on the stage many times, never have I felt so wracked with nerves. Matthew is snoring, so at least Hamlet's mother is getting some sleep.

11 May 1601

The day of the first performance has arrived and it begins in an hour or two's time. I am snatching a moment to write in my diary and to calm myself. Already I can hear the theatre's musicians marching up and down in the street outside, drumming and trumpeting to draw people in for the show. The flag is flying on the roof of the Globe to signal that the play will soon begin. It is flapping against a dull sky, but we hope that rain will keep off until tonight.

Meanwhile I say a little prayer: Lord, help me make Ophelia truly come to life before she meets her sorry death.

12 MAY 1601

Yesterday was surely the most extraordinary day ever seen in the theatre. Life and art came together, mixed and exploded like a magician's potion! Let me set the scene for you. With Mr Burbage's help Sir John Crosse had secretly stationed his disguised, but armed, men throughout the theatre. His agents had replaced our usual doormen and stood by the theatre entrances with the entrance money boxes. Meanwhile, up in the Lords' Room behind the stage, important-looking gentlemen sat murmuring and flashing their jewels, and I had no doubt that one or two of those were really working for Sir John.

Down on the ground below the stage, and in the galleries, I believed there were more disguised Queen's agents, perhaps among the orange and nut sellers walking round with their trays. But imagine my surprise when I saw a familiar face amongst the fashionably-bearded young gallants sitting in the nearest, most expensive, gallery seats smoking the latest pipes and wisecracking with each other. It was none other than Sir John Crosse himself, outdoing the others at playing the empty-headed young dandy whose only talent is blowing smoke rings.

All in all the crowd looked a prosperous

happy-go-lucky lot, a good bait for the would-be pickpockets who were already in amongst the crowd somewhere, I was sure.

Music announced that the play was to begin, and a hush descended as Mr Burbage began a powerful performance as Hamlet. William Shakespeare's words flowed from him as naturally and as smoothly as a glittering stream of water. I was Ophelia, driven mad by her beloved Hamlet's behaviour, with no power and no way of escaping a horrible fate. Part of the way through the play Ophelia's death by drowning was announced on stage:

"Alas, then is she drowned?"
"Drowned, drowned."

My part was finished and I stood backstage in the tiring-room, feeling great relief that I had got through the part.

At the very end most of the characters were dead, so their "bodies" were taken offstage. A signal shot was fired from a cannon positioned on the roof of the theatre, and so *Hamlet* ended. But my story does not. The crowd hailed the new play noisily. They obviously loved it. In the confusion that followed I saw Sir John Crosse spring up and give a signal; then shouts rose above the hubbub.

"Seize them!"
"Seize the pickpockets!"

The Queen's agents grabbed several men on the ground and in the galleries. Some struggled but were soon subdued.

"Don't panic. Nothing is amiss," I heard Sir John's voice calming the crowd. "No need to panic. No need."

Out of the corner of my eye I saw two of the gang I recognised from the inn. They leapt up the stairs to the Lords' Room, only to be overpowered by the gentlemen waiting there.

Then suddenly the tiring-room door burst open. The scarred man had reached it in his effort to escape capture. His eyes glittered with hate when he saw me cornered, with no way out.

"You! You miserable little traitor! I recognised you in that scruffy woman's get-up, your hair all askew. In spite of your wig and all your fine petticoats I know you for the whey-faced snoop I have been watching at the Blue Boar! You have betrayed us, you damned smooth-faced boy!" His dagger flicked into his hand.

"Ophelia indeed! You shall die by drowning, for certain! This time in your own blood!"

He advanced towards me and I was trapped in a corner. I tried to shield myself with my arms but felt myself sliding down the wall as blood splattered on to the floor around me.

The blood was not mine, though it took me a minute to realise it. It belonged to the scarred man, now lying crumpled on the floor in front of me, his head split by a blow from behind. Thomas the tireman had picked up the skull prop and smashed it down hard on his head.

"A fine performance!" Thomas cried, addressing the bloodstained skull. Then Sir John Crosse burst in, followed by his men. "Will, thank goodness you aren't harmed. We have caught them all, their pockets stuffed with other people's property. This villain looks all but finished."

We looked down at the man on the floor, his scar now a rivulet of blood. I felt sick and began to sway, and Sir John caught me as I fell in a faint. He was wearing a pendant filled with sweet-smelling spices, and he brought me round by wafting it beneath my nose.

"It seems you have learnt something today, Will. The theatre is a magical place indeed, but life is a much more brutal affair where death is all too real." He spoke quietly as he helped me to sit up. "One day you may be called on to play a dying man, and this lesson will serve you when you need to show his pain and anguish."

I saw Shakespeare standing in the doorway, listening and silently taking in the scene. Then he turned and walked away.

2 JUNE 1601

The sun is shining softly today and London is at its best, I think, before the summer heat. The crowds are pouring into the Globe, eight hundred people a day, to see Hamlet meet his sorry end. I hope that they shed a tear for my Ophelia, too.

Tomorrow I am to appear somewhere else – in court to act as a witness against the gang of thieves.

4 JUNE 1601

When I was called into the law court yesterday, I saw the remaining gang members sitting in front of me. I told my story to the court as best I could, but I had to use all the stage experience I knew to master my nerves. Those accused men were the most hostile audience I have ever had. Pure hatred flared in their eyes and they reminded me most of the maddened bear-baiting dogs I had come across the night I hid in the bear's barn.

My evidence was not the only tale to be told. Others bore witness to the gang's many different crimes and they were condemned to be hanged. Their bodies will be left rotting by the roadside to warn others against stealing.

It did not make me feel triumphant. Instead, I remembered Sir John Crosse's words: "Life is a brutal affair, where death is all too real."

6 JUNE 1601

Mr Burbage and Mr Heminges have spoken to me about my future, as my apprenticeship is very nearly over. Mr Heminges began by patting me on the shoulder. "Your voice will soon break, Will, and then women's roles will no longer be open to you. Do you want to try for adult male roles, and continue your life in the theatre? Boy actors have tried to cross over to work as adult players before, not always successfully, it is true. But we think you have the talent. You have shown much of it in these last few weeks, not only as Ophelia, but in your performances for Sir John Crosse. I am proud of you, my boy."

Mr Burbage was also encouraging: "The Chamberlain's Men will be pleased to try you out again next season, Will. Your voice may be lower but not your acting abilities. In the meantime, a band of us will be going on tour to

Scotland this summer, and you are welcome to come. To tell the truth, the Queen must soon choose an heir to her throne and it is most likely to be James of Scotland. We want to go north to show him our talents. In short, we want him to be our supporter when the time comes for him to sit on the throne. Think about it, Will."

Meanwhile, Matthew has decided to leave acting, and I shall miss him sorely. "Don't worry; I'll write to you," he said, "I've enjoyed being a boy actor but I don't think I'm good enough to make it a lifetime career. Besides, I want to travel and see new lands. Unknown treasures, marvellous beasts… They're all out there and I want to find them! They say America is the land of plenty, so I think I'll try to work my passage out there and see for myself."

So, what shall I do? Go home to the apothecary shop or try for a life in the theatre? Well, I think you know the answer. I must at least try, for those who do not try are bound to fail. I will visit Scotland with the Chamberlain's Men, but first I am going to take a detour and ride to Marlborough on an important mission. I have a precious treasure to deliver, after all. Wrapped carefully in my saddlebag there will be a diary written especially for you, my dear sister Judith. Keep it always as a momento of your dear brother, the actor.

7 June 1601

Her Majesty's Palace of Whitehall

To William Savage,

As a reward for your true service to Her Majesty Queen Elizabeth, and her grateful subjects, the Queen's humble servants have been ordered to have your unfinished portrait completed and ensure it is delivered to the Globe Theatre for you.

Sir John Crosse

ELIZABETHAN THEATRE

ACTING CHILDREN

Some popular Elizabethan acting companies were made up entirely of children, ranging from the age of eight to about thirteen. They did a lot of singing and dancing in their productions, and we know they performed plays for the Queen.

STAYING YOUNG LONGER

Scholars think that, because of their different diet, Elizabethan boys reached puberty later than boys do now, and their voices broke around the age of sixteen or seventeen. That is why Will Savage is called a boy in our story, even though he is sixteen.

WRITING PLAYS DOWN

Once a new play was written as a manuscript by a playwright, someone at the theatre had to copy it out to make one more precious copy which was owned by the theatre and used for prompting. Then, each actor was given their own part written out separately and stuck on a parchment roll. No actor had a full version of the play.

PROPS

Elizabethan theatres didn't have big pieces of scenery, but the actors did use props to help them (for instance, the skull in *Hamlet*).

A NOISY CROWD

Nobody is certain exactly what an Elizabethan stage looked like, but historians have a fairly good idea from old drawings and descriptions. We know that audiences could pay a penny to stand and more to sit in the galleries. The audience could easily give their comments to the actors. See pages 82-83.

BACKSTAGE

Backstage was called the tiring house. The space was used as the dressing room and to store props. Actors could be raised and lowered on to the stage from a ceiling above the stage. The ceiling was painted with the moon, stars and sun. The whole theatre was brightly painted.

OFF STAGE AND ON

There was no stage curtain. Instead, actors went in and out of doors to come on stage or leave it. Shakespeare did not divide his plays into acts or scenes, as we do now. That was done later on.

MUSIC

Theatre companies had their own musicians. Plays usually began and ended with music.

LIGHTING

There was no lighting at the Globe, so the plays had to be performed in daylight. When plays were performed indoors, candles were used.

TIMELINE OF SHAKESPEARE'S LIFE

This timeline shows some of the information we have about Shakespeare's life, plus some important dates in theatre history.

1564

- William Shakespeare is born in Stratford, Warwickshire.

1582

- Shakespeare marries Anne Hathaway.

1583

- A daughter, Susanna, is born.

1585

- Twins Hamnet and Judith are born.

1595

- Shakespeare is in London and performs in front of the Queen.

1596

- His son Hamnet dies, aged eleven.

1597

- He buys a large house in Stratford.

1599

- The Globe Theatre is opened. Shakespeare takes a share in the ownership and writes plays for the company. Orsino, the Italian count, visits Queen Elizabeth.

1601

- The Earl of Essex's rebellion fails and he is executed. Shakespeare uses Orsino's name for a character in *Twelfth Night*. He writes *Hamlet*.

1603

- Queen Elizabeth I dies and James I becomes king. Theatres are closed by the plague until April 1604, by which time 30,000 Londoners have died.

1604

- Shakespeare's success is at its height, but he spends more time in Stratford than London.

1605

- The first stage scenery is used in an English performance (at court).

1608

- The Chamberlain's Men (now renamed the King's Men) open an indoor theatre at Blackfriars, but keep the Globe Theatre open.

1613

- The Globe Theatre burns to the ground but is rebuilt and reopened.

1616

- Shakespeare dies at Stratford.

GLOSSARY

ACTING COMPANY
A group of actors who were given an official licence to perform plays. No group without a licence was allowed to act.

APOTHECARY
A kind of chemist who made medicines from ingredients such as herbs and roots.

APPRENTICE
A boy who was learning a trade.

BANKSIDE
The area on the south bank of the Thames.

BEAR-BAITING
Bears or bulls were chained in an arena called a bear-baiting pit or bear garden and attacked by dogs in front of a crowd.

CITY OF LONDON
Area inside the city walls on the north bank of the Thames.

GALLERIES
Seating set around the walls of a theatre.

GROUNDLINGS
Spectators who stood in front of the stage.

LONDON BRIDGE

The only bridge across the River Thames in London during Elizabethan times.

LORDS' ROOM

Private theatre seating for grand people.

PATRON

A rich and influential supporter.

PLAYER

The Elizabethan name for an actor.

PROMPTER

Someone who sits by the stage and reminds actors of their lines if they forget them.

PROPS

Objects used by the actors during a play.

SHARERS

The people who owned shares in the Globe Theatre. They helped pay to put on plays, and took part of the profits.

TIREMAN

Someone who looked after the costumes and props backstage.

TIRING-ROOM, THE

The backstage dressing-room, where props, copies of plays and costumes were kept.

Other titles in this series

The diary of a Young Roman Soldier

Marcus Gallo travels to Britain with his legion to help pacify the wild Celtic tribes.

The diary of a Young Tudor Lady-in-Waiting

Young Rebecca Swann joins her aunt as a lady-in-waiting at the court of Queen Elizabeth the First.

The diary of a Victorian Apprentice

Samuel Cobbett becomes an apprentice at a factory making steam locomotives.

The diary of a Young Nurse in World War II

Jean Harris is hired to train as a nurse in a London hospital just as World War II breaks out.

The diary of a Young Soldier in World War I

Billy Warren and his mates have signed up to go to France and fight in World War I.

The diary of a Young West Indian Immigrant

Gloria Charles travels from Dominica in the West Indies to start a new life in Britain.

The diary of a 1960s Teenager

Teenager Jane Leachman is offered a job working in swinging London's fashion industry.